TERRIERS AND TIARAS REUNION

Starring

ZOE TRENT

Written by Ellie O'Ryan

Ⓛ Ⓑ

Little, Brown and Company
New York Boston

Little, Brown and Company

Hachette Book Group
1290 Avenue of the Americas, New York, NY 10104
Visit us at lb-kids.com

Little, Brown and Company is a division of Hachette Book Group, Inc. The Little, Brown name and logo are trademarks of Hachette Book Group, Inc.

The publisher is not responsible for websites (or their content) that are not owned by the publisher.

First Edition: October 2015

ISBN 978-0-316-30136-7

10 9 8 7 6 5 4 3 2 1

RRD-C

Printed in the United States of America

For Rebecca Caroline Hosek and
Josephine Keely Hosek

CONTENTS

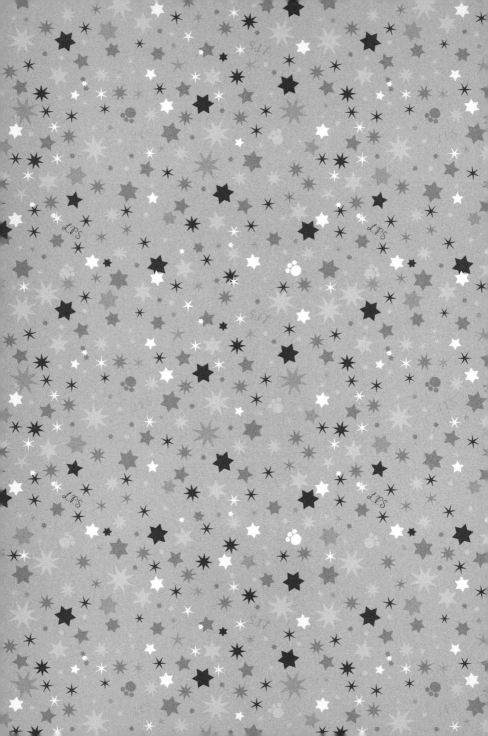

Chapter 1

The sun was streaming through the windows of the Littlest Pet Shop. It was a beautiful Saturday morning, and Blythe Baxter was hanging out with her favorite pals—the pets who came to Day Camp at the best pet store in all of Downtown City.

"What are you working on, Blythe?" asked

Zoe, a Cavalier King Charles spaniel who had style to spare.

"I'm not sure yet," Blythe admitted as she reached for a purple colored pencil. She carefully started shading in her latest fashion design—a frilly skirt and lacy scarf that would be perfect for a dog like Zoe.

"Well, you might not know what it is, but I know that I like it," Zoe told her. "In fact, I *love* it!"

Blythe grinned. "Thanks, Zoe," she said. "When my new fabric arrives, it will be easier to figure out if this design will work or not."

Ring-a-ling!

Everyone looked up as Lewis, the neighborhood letter carrier, walked through the door of the Littlest Pet Shop.

"*Ooh*, maybe it's already here!" Zoe said excitedly.

But all Lewis heard was *yip-yip-yip-yip-yip!*

"Easy, girl," he said, glancing at Zoe out of the corner of his eye. "I don't know what it is about dogs, Blythe. They all seem to hate the mailman."

Blythe tried to hide her smile. "Oh no. Zoe doesn't hate you," she assured Lewis. "I think she's just excited to see you."

Being able to communicate with animals was one of Blythe's many talents, and she was determined to keep it a secret. She couldn't imagine what would happen If people ever realized that all those yips, yowls, squawks, and meows were really words! When Blythe got over the shock of realizing that she could communicate with her animal friends, she knew how lucky she was to understand what the animals were saying.

"And I'm glad you're here, too! Any

packages for me today?" Blythe continued as Lewis placed his mailbag on the counter.

"Well, I'm not sure," Lewis said as he dug around in his bag. "Are you expecting… a special delivery express package from 2 Cute Fabrics Incorporated?" he asked.

"Yes!" Blythe squealed. "My fabric order! It's finally here!"

Just then, Mrs. Twombly, the owner of the Littlest Pet Shop, returned from the stockroom. "I don't know, Blythe," she said, sounding a little worried. "We're running awfully low on Pampered Pet Gourmet Snacks and—"

At that moment, Mrs. Twombly noticed Lewis. A grin spread across her face. "Oh! Perfect timing!" she exclaimed. "Is there a delivery from the Pampered Pet Company?"

Lewis nodded. "Several cases, ma'am,"

he told her. "If you'd just step outside to sign for delivery, I think I've got everything you need on the truck."

While Blythe opened her package, Zoe took a peek at the rest of the mail. Among all the boring white envelopes, a colorful postcard stood out. "Hey, Blythe—what's that?" she asked.

"Looks like a postcard," Blythe replied. "I wonder who it's from."

Blythe crossed the room and started to read the note. When she gasped, all the pets turned to look at her.

"What is it? What's wrong?" Russell the hedgehog asked anxiously. He might have been prickly on the outside, but inside, he was all heart.

For a moment, Blythe didn't answer, but when she looked up from the card, a huge smile was plastered on her face. "Nothing's wrong," she said. "In fact, everything's perfect! Remember when *Terriers and Tiaras* filmed an episode in Downtown City?"

All the pets nodded. How could they forget when the hit reality show *Terriers and Tiaras* came to town? It had been one of the wildest weeks ever, especially when Zoe had begged Blythe to accompany her on the show. Zoe felt like her dreams of being a reality TV star had finally come true! But it turned out that being on a reality show wasn't a dream at all. It was more like a nightmare. And as the cameras kept rolling, the truth finally came out: The prizewinning pooches on the show weren't interested in constantly competing. They just wanted to make friends and have fun, not primp and perform all day long. Even

Zoe decided that reality TV shows, with all their made-up drama and bad feelings, were not for her. When she quit, the other famous pooches followed her lead. And they'd never been happier!

"Well, we've just received a postcard from Philippa and P.S.!" Blythe continued excitedly.

Minka, a mischievous monkey and artist extraordinaire, looked confused. "P.S.?" she asked.

"P.S. is Princess Stori's new name, remember?" Zoe reminded her. Princess Stori was the most famous dog on *Terriers and Tiaras*—and the one with the worst owner, too. Judi Jo Jameson cared about one thing and one thing only: winning. In fact, Princess Stori wasn't even a girl dog—he was a boy! When he met Zoe, Princess Stori had walked away from the show, his old name, and even Judi Jo. Now everyone knew him as P.S., and he had a great life with Judi Jo's former assistant, Philippa.

Blythe held up the postcard so everyone could see the picture on it. " 'Dear Blythe,' " she read. " 'How are you? I have some exciting news. P.S. and I are taking a cross-country road trip...and we're going to stop in Downtown City! We can't wait to see you and Zoe! Love, Philippa.' "

Blythe turned the postcard over and showed the pets the back. "There's even a paw print from P.S. at the bottom," she added.

"A P.S. from P.S.!" joked Pepper, a silly skunk who always kept the rest of the pets laughing.

Zoe flashed her most dazzling smile.

"This is the best news ever!" she cried. "I can't *wait* to see P.S. and Philippa again. If only the rest of our *Terriers and Tiaras* pals could visit, too."

"That would be so cool," Blythe agreed. "Like a reunion!"

Zoe's eyes grew wide. "You're a genius, Blythe!" she exclaimed. "We simply *have* to invite Shea Butter and Sam U.L., too!"

Blythe reached for her phone. "That's a great idea, Zoe!" she replied. "I'll e-mail their owners right now to see if they can come."

"Wait a second..." Zoe said as a brilliant idea popped into her head. "If everybody's going to be together again, maybe we could do more than have a reunion. Maybe... maybe... maybe we could put on a show!"

For the first time, Blythe's smile faded. "A...show?" she asked slowly. "I don't know,

Zoe. Don't you remember what happened last time?"

Everyone cringed a little—especially Blythe. Since Zoe's owners were out of town for the filming of *Terriers and Tiaras*, Blythe had served as Zoe's handler at the show. She had transformed into one of the most demanding, pushy, intense dog-show moms of all time! The pets had been totally baffled by the change in Blythe. One minute, she was her regular self—kind, sweet, caring, and ready for fun, but after spending time around P.S.'s former owner, pageant queen Judi Jo, Blythe only wanted to win—no matter what. Luckily, Blythe realized that she was going about it all wrong... and everybody could tell that Blythe never wanted to let a show affect her caring personality again!

"That won't happen this time," Zoe assured her. "We *all* learned what was really important."

"Staying away from hot curling irons and super-sticky fake-eyelash glue?" Pepper joked.

Zoe scrunched up her face as everyone laughed. "No!" she replied—but she couldn't help joining in the laughter. "We learned that it's more important to have fun with our friends than to get obsessed with winning a silly pageant. This time, the show will be all fun and no pressure. I promise."

"But what if I get carried away again?" Blythe asked, sounding worried.

"You won't," Zoe said firmly. "This show won't be about winning or losing. It will be about performing and sharing talents! And this time, *everyone* gets a chance to have their time to shine onstage."

The other pets looked surprised.

"Even me?" squeaked Sunil the mongoose. He wasn't quite sure if this was something he needed to worry about yet, but when it came to worrying, Sunil believed that it was never too early to start.

"And me?" added Vinnie the gecko. Vinnie and Sunil were best friends, but unlike Sunil, Vinnie didn't spend much time worrying. He'd rather work on his dancing skills—and play with his pals.

"Everyone who wants to," Zoe declared. "We'll—"

The Littlest Pet Shop erupted into such loud cheers that no one could hear what else Zoe had to say.

"Okay, okay, I give in," Blythe said, holding up her hands. When the pets finally quieted down, Blythe continued. "On one condition."

Zoe's ears pricked up. She could already tell that whatever Blythe had to say was important.

"Zoe, I want you to be in charge of the show," Blythe told her in a serious voice.

"Me?" Zoe asked in astonishment. *"Me?"*

"I'm happy to make the costumes and help out however I can, but if I'm in charge, I might start bossing everybody around again, and nobody wants that," Blythe explained. "So if you—"

"Yes, yes, yes, yes!" Zoe cried excitedly. "Thank you, Blythe! I know I can do this. First, we'll need a place to have the show..."

"What about here?" suggested Penny Ling, a gentle, graceful panda.

"That might work," Zoe said. "Or maybe… the Pawza Hotel."

"Wonderful idea!" Sunil exclaimed. "Their new lounge is opening soon. My owner was talking about it last night. He said it's got a stage and a runway and about a zillion shiny lights!"

"Just imagine it!" Zoe breathed. "We could build the most amazing set…"

"Yes!" Russell exclaimed.

"And paint it with all kinds of shimmery, glittery paints…" continued Zoe.

"Magnificent!" Minka spoke up.

"Maybe we could even be the new lounge's opening night act!" Zoe cried. Then she shook her head. "I'm getting ahead of myself. First, we've got to invite everybody else. Blythe, would you e-mail their owners for me?"

"On it!" Blythe replied as she grabbed her phone. Her fingers flew across the screen as she tapped out an e-mail.

TO: tanya.twitchel@paw.com, cindeanna.mellon@paw.com

CC: philippa@paw.com

SUBJECT: Terriers and Tiaras Reunion Show!

Hey, everybody! Exciting news—Philippa and P.S. will be visiting Downtown City, and we're hoping you can visit, too! It would be so great to have a *Terriers and Tiaras* Reunion, but it wouldn't be complete without you and your pups. We can even put on a show! LMK if you can come. See you soon (we hope!!!).

Love,
Blythe and your pet friends at the Littlest Pet Shop

When Blythe finished typing, she read the e-mail aloud. "How does that sound?" she asked Zoe.

"Perfect," Zoe replied, her eyes shining with joy.

Blythe tapped her phone to send the e-mail to Sam U.L.'s and Shea Butter's owners. "Now I'm going to call the Pawza Hotel to see if we can book the stage for our show," she announced.

Zoe was so excited she felt like dancing. The *Terriers and Tiaras* Reunion Show was officially happening.

Which meant that it was time to get to work!

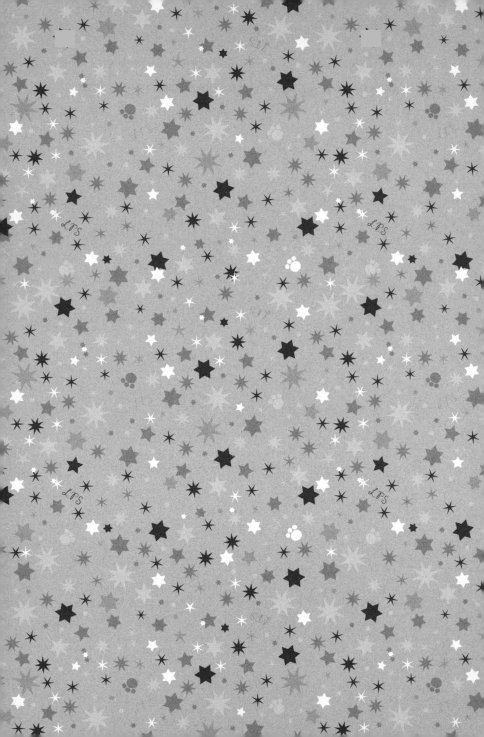

Chapter 2

"Pet huddle!" Zoe announced. She led everybody into the Day Camp section of the Littlest Pet Shop—a large comfortable room with everything from games and toys to slides and activities. Not only was there plenty of room for the pets to work on their favorite hobbies, there were also dozens of comfy cushions and cozy beds that were just right for hanging out or napping.

Zoe grinned at the other pets as they gathered around her. It felt good to be in charge. In fact, Zoe was pretty sure she could get used to it.

"If we're going to put on a show, we have to start practicing now," Zoe told her friends. "P.S., Sam U.L., and Shea Butter have tons of experience being in shows. We don't want to look silly onstage with a bunch of professionals. Does anybody know which talent they'd like to perform in the show?"

Penny Ling raised her paw. "Maybe I could do a new routine with my ribbon stick," she said. "Something with lots of twirling and tumbling. I even have a shiny new ribbon I could use!"

"That sounds perfect!" Zoe exclaimed. "The twirlier, the better!"

"People love to laugh," Pepper spoke up. "I've been practicing my mime routine. There's a really funny part where I pretend that I'm being chased by a giant banana."

Minka's eyes lit up. "A giant banana? I *wish* we had one of those! Can you even imagine the enormous banana split we could make?" she said.

Zoe giggled. "That would be tasty," she said. "Anyway, Pepper, I love that idea—it sounds hilarious! Now, Vinnie and Sunil— what about you guys?"

Sunil popped his top hat on his head. "Magic, of course!" he exclaimed. "I have a brand-new top secret trick that's ready for the spotlight."

Zoe grinned. "I had a feeling you would," she said. "And how about you, Vinnie?"

"Hmm…" he said thoughtfully. "How about a dance routine? I can show off all my best moves."

"Great!" Zoe said. "Start practicing right away, my friends. I can't wait to see your routines when they're ready!"

As Penny Ling, Pepper, Sunil, and Vinnie scurried off, Zoe realized that Russell and Minka were still standing there. "Oops! We can't forget about you two," she told them. "What do you want to do in the show? I can help you think of an act, if you want."

Russell and Minka exchanged a glance. "Um, Zoe, I'm not sure that being onstage is the best job for me," said Russell.

"But, Russell! When all the dogs walked off the show, *you* won the crown," Zoe reminded him. "Remember? How could we put on a *Terriers and Tiaras* Reunion Show without *you*?"

"Yeah…well…once was enough," Russell said sheepishly, remembering his moment in the spotlight after all the dogs left to have some fun. "But I still want to be a part of everything, even if I'm not onstage. Don't *you* need a helper?"

A tiny frown crossed Zoe's face. *A helper?* she wondered. *Doesn't Russell think I can handle it?*

"Blythe's making costumes, but what about building the set?" Russell continued.

"Oh!" Zoe exclaimed as relief washed over her. "Of course. I didn't even *think* about the set. We'll definitely need someone to design and build it, Russell. Thanks! That's a great job for you!"

"And I can paint it!" Minka suggested. "And make some posters, too, so we can advertise the show to everybody in Downtown City."

"You two are the best," Zoe said. "I can't wait to see what you come up with!"

"Big news, everybody," Blythe announced as she joined them. "Our show plans have come at the best possible time. The entertainment for the opening-night celebration of the Pawza Hotel's new lounge canceled this morning. The manager there was panicking about finding a replacement!"

"Really?" gasped Zoe.

"Really!" Blythe told her. "He thinks your idea for a *Terriers and Tiaras* Reunion Show is fantastic. And he predicted that you'll be performing to a sold-out audience!"

"A sold-out audience..." Zoe repeated

dreamily. She could just picture it: an excited human sitting in every seat...holding an even more excited pet...the entire crowd leaping up for a standing ovation at the end of the show...the shining spotlight as everybody onstage took a bow...

And suddenly, right in the middle of the world's best daydream, Zoe had another idea.

"Blythe!" she sputtered excitedly. "What if we sell tickets to the show? All the profits can go to the Downtown City Animal Shelter to help the pets there find their forever homes!"

"Wow, Zoe," replied Blythe. "That's such a generous idea! I love it!"

"Hold everything!" Zoe cried.

All the activity came to a halt as the pets spun around to look at Zoe.

"Oops." She giggled. "I mean, carry on, everybody. Minka!"

The little monkey scampered up to Zoe with a paintbrush behind her ear. "At your service!" she chattered.

"Minka, we've got to start making the posters right now," Zoe said. "The earlier we advertise, the more tickets we can sell, and that means more money raised for the animal shelter."

"I'll call the hotel manager to tell him about your plan," Blythe said.

"We want the posters to be dazzling," Zoe told Minka. "Bright colors, big words— Blythe will write those, of course—"

Before Zoe could even finish telling Minka what she wanted to see on the posters, the monkey zoomed away. Minka was just a blur as she zipped around the Littlest

Pet Shop, gathering everything she would need for the posters: poster board, paint, markers, and lots of glitter. Zoe couldn't wait to see what Minka would come up with!

About an hour later, Minka unveiled the very first poster. "What do you think? What do you think?" she asked eagerly as she hopped from one foot to the other.

Zoe stepped closer to take a better look. "Oh, Minka!" she gasped. "It's beautiful!"

Around the edges of the poster, Minka had drawn long red curtains—the kind that hang in theaters. A bright yellow spotlight shone down onto a stage, with plenty of glitter so that it reflected the light, just like a real spotlight. Standing right in the middle of the spotlight was a drawing of... Zoe herself!

"Did I leave enough room for the letters?" Minka asked anxiously.

"Oh, definitely," Zoe assured her. "I *love* this design, Minka! It's too perfect! Now for the other posters. Can you make one with P.S. standing in the spotlight? And one with Sam U.L.? And one with—"

"Let me guess: Shea Butter," Minka said with a giggle. "Sure, Zoe, I think I can handle that."

"Awesome poster, Minka!" Blythe exclaimed as she joined them. Then she turned to Zoe. "Have you figured out what you want me to write?"

Zoe looked thoughtful for a moment. "How about…'*Terriers and Tiaras* Reunion' at the top, in giant letters," she suggested. "Maybe Minka can draw a big star on the bottom of the poster, and you could write a different pet's name on each one. You know, P.S., Shea Butter..."

Blythe raised her eyebrows. "But we haven't heard back from anybody yet," she reminded Zoe. "If the others can't come, we can still put on a show, but we can't call it a *Terriers and Tiaras* Reunion without them."

"They'll be here," Zoe said confidently. "I know they will. My friends wouldn't miss it for the world!"

"But—" Blythe began. Then she stopped herself. "Sorry, Zoe. You're in charge. Whatever you say goes."

"Thanks, Blythe," Zoe said. "I'm sure we'll sell more tickets if people know they have a chance to see P.S., Shea Butter, and Sam U.L. in person!"

"And you, of course!" added Minka.

Blythe reached for one of Minka's markers and started carefully writing the words in her best handwriting. Seeing the finished poster made Zoe so happy she almost started chasing her tail in glee, just like a puppy!

Chapter 3

For the next few days, the Littlest Pet Shop was buzzing with activity. Every moment of Day Camp was dedicated to behind-the-scenes planning for Russell, Minka, and Blythe, and nonstop rehearsals for the performing pets. From the *clackity-clackity-clackity-whirrrrr* of Blythe's sewing machine as she worked on the costumes to the *bang-bang-bang* of Russell's hammer as he built the set, there was so much noise that Zoe could barely hear herself think. But Zoe didn't mind. She knew that all that activity would lead to one thing: the very best show that Downtown City had ever seen! With her extra-special director accessories—a folding chair and clipboard—Zoe felt like she had everything under control.

Russell and Minka had spent hours designing the set. The busy little hedgehog had already built dozens of wooden stars. Whenever Russell finished a star, Minka decorated it with glimmering gold paint. When all the stars were painted, Russell planned to nail them together so that each star overlapped just a bit. Zoe cocked her head as she stared at the shimmery stars that Minka had propped up against the wall to dry. *It's a good start*, Zoe thought. *But something's missing.*

Zoe realized that Russell and Minka were eagerly waiting to hear what she thought of their work.

"You've both done a wonderful job!" Zoe told them. "The set design couldn't *possibly* be better…unless…"

Russell and Minka sat up a little straighter. "What is it? What's wrong?" Russell asked anxiously.

"Oh, goodness, Russell, nothing's *wrong*, exactly," Zoe said as she searched for the right words. The last thing she wanted to do was hurt their feelings, especially when they were working so hard. "It's just…well…all that gold paint…I wonder if the stars will stand out enough if they're all painted the exact same color, especially to people who are sitting in the back of the lounge."

Minka scampered across the room to look at the stars from a distance. "Wow, Zoe, you're right!" she exclaimed. "What are we going to do?"

"We could add some silver stars," suggested Russell.

"Yes, perfect!" Zoe said. "Or stars in all different colors...like a rainbow galaxy. I really love the shimmery paint you're using, Minka. It makes the set look so fancy."

"Shimmery rainbow paint. Got it," Minka shouted as she rushed off to get more art supplies. Soon, the work area was filled with a dozen different paint cans and brushes. As Minka added purple paint to one of the stars, Zoe breathed a sigh of relief. *Problem solved!* she thought happily.

"You have great ideas, Zoe," Russell said with admiration. "How'd you get to be so good at directing?"

"That's really nice of you, Russell, but to be honest, I'm just figuring it out as I go," Zoe admitted. "I don't even know what I'm doing!"

"Well, you saved the set. That's for sure!" Russell told her as he picked up his hammer again.

Zoe should have been happy, but there was a strange feeling of worry tugging at her. *What if I hadn't noticed that the stars were all blending together?* she wondered. *What if I'd missed it completely? What if... what if there are other things I'm missing?*

There was only one thing to do: call an immediate meeting to check on everyone else's progress.

Zoe, perched in her director's chair and feeling *very* official, clapped her paws together. "Attention, everyone!" she said in her best take-charge voice. "I'd like to see how your acts are coming along for the entertainment part of our show. So come on down and show me what you've got!"

"*Ooh*, I just *love* dress rehearsals!" Penny Ling gushed as she grabbed her ribbon stick.

"A dress rehearsal?" Blythe gulped. "Um, Zoe...don't we need costumes for that? I'm nowhere *near* ready!"

"Don't worry, Blythe," Zoe assured her. "It's not a dress rehearsal exactly...not yet, anyway. We'll have a dress rehearsal the night before the show. For now, I just want to see a preview of each act."

"Phew!" Blythe sighed, looking relieved. "Well, back to the sewing machine for me."

"Blythe, hold on," Zoe said, putting a paw on Blythe's ankle. "I was hoping you'd stay and help me with the rehearsal. Do you want to bring your sketches? We can see how each costume matches up with each act."

"I could use some help, too," Penny Ling spoke up. "Blythe, would you turn on my music?"

"And I need someone to introduce me," added Pepper as she quickly smeared some white makeup on her face—just like a real mime.

"I think I can handle that," Blythe told them as she pulled up a chair next to Zoe. "It's probably a good idea to give my sewing machine a little break, too."

Zoe checked her clipboard. "Penny Ling, you're up," she announced.

Penny Ling stood very still in the middle of the stage as Blythe started the music. When the first few notes played, Penny Ling stretched out her right arm, with the ribbon stick clutched tightly in her paw. With a graceful motion, Penny Ling brought the ribbon over her head in a wide arc—just like a rainbow. Zoe sucked in her breath as Penny Ling started to twirl, making the ribbon dance along with her.

"Here's what I'm thinking for Penny Ling's costume," Blythe whispered as she passed her sketchbook over to Zoe.

It was hard to look away from the fluttering ribbon, but Zoe stole a glance at Blythe's sketch—a fluttery skirt with lace trim that perfectly matched Penny Ling's ribbon. "Gorgeous!" Zoe told Blythe.

When Penny Ling's routine ended, Pepper took the stage. With a twinkle in her eye, Pepper pointed at her open mouth but didn't make a sound.

"That's my cue!" Blythe exclaimed as she scrambled up from her chair. She cleared her throat and proclaimed, "Ladies and gentlemen, it is my pleasure to introduce Pepper the mime!"

Soon all the pets were cracking up as Pepper first pretended to peel a banana, and then slipped and fell all over the stage. When she pretended the banana was chasing her, Vinnie laughed so hard he fell over!

"Okay, Sunil, your turn!" Zoe called out

when she finally caught her breath. "I can't wait to find out which trick you're going to perform."

The mongoose looked at her with his big eyes as he shook his head. "Oh no, a magician never reveals his secrets!" he exclaimed.

Zoe frowned. "But...don't you want to practice in front of everybody?" she asked.

Sunil shook his head again. "And ruin the surprise? Never!" he said firmly.

Zoe and Blythe exchanged a glance. Blythe could tell that Zoe wasn't sure what to do. "It's up to you," Blythe said in a quiet voice. "You're the director."

Zoe thought about it for a moment. *I guess I could insist that Sunil show me his magic trick*, she thought. *But I promised that our show would be all about fun, and not about stress and pressure.*

"Okay, Sunil," Zoe finally said. "If you want to keep your trick top secret until the show, that's fine with me. Just let me know if you need any help."

Sunil flashed her a giant grin. "Thanks, Zoe!" he said as he scampered back to his magic station. "I promise you won't be disappointed!"

I hope he's right, Zoe thought as she peeked at her clipboard. "Let's see...who's next?"

"Me!" shouted Vinnie as he leaped in front of her. "I guess you saved the best for last, huh, Zoe?"

Zoe laughed. "Let's see what you've got," she replied.

"Hit it, Blythe!" Vinnie called. Blythe started the music, Vinnie started dancing, and Zoe's smile started to fade. Vinnie was, well, there was only one way to put it: Vinnie was *terrible*! Every move he made was sloppy and uncoordinated. He wasn't dancing to the beat, either. And he even forgot some steps! From the expression on Blythe's face, Zoe could tell she agreed.

Zoe tried to look on the bright side. *Vinnie loves to dance,* she reminded herself. *Maybe he'll let me give him some suggestions. A little choreography . . . some simple routines . . . yes! We can do this!*

"Zoe! Zoe! Pay attention!" Vinnie called from the stage. "It's time for my big finish!"

"I'm watching, Vinnie!" Zoe called back. She held her breath as Vinnie backed up, started running, took a flying leap…and crashed right into Minka's paint cans!

Bang! Clatter! Crash! Smash!

The racket was so loud that all the pets spun around to look. They found Vinnie sitting right in the middle of a rainbow puddle of paint that was spreading across the floor. The paint had splattered everywhere—even on Minka and Russell!

"Oh no!" Minka shrieked as Russell frantically wiped his prickly quills. "My paints!"

"Oops," Vinnie muttered. "That wasn't supposed to happen."

Just then, Mrs. Twombly peeked in. "Is everything okay? I thought I heard…" she began. Her eyes grew wide as she spotted the mess. "Oh, gracious! Hold on—let me go start the bathwater."

"Whoa," whispered Zoe as Mrs. Twombly hurried off to get baths ready for Russell, Minka, and Vinnie. Then, in a louder voice, she said, "Okay, everybody, we can handle this! Pepper, get some mops. Sunil, you're on soap. Penny Ling, find some sponges. We'll get this mess cleaned up and then we'll all break for lunch. I think we've earned it."

As everyone scurried around to start cleaning the mess, Zoe hurried over to Vinnie. She held out a paw to help him up.

"That was a big finish, all right," Zoe joked, but Vinnie wasn't even able to crack a smile.

"I don't know what went wrong, Zoe," he replied glumly. "I made a mess of everything!"

"Dancing isn't easy, Vinnie," she told him. "Professional dancers have to practice for *years* to get their moves just right."

"But I don't have years," Vinnie said. "The show is in a few days. Maybe I should quit. I don't want to make a mess of the show, too."

Oh no, Zoe thought. *I made Vinnie feel even worse!* Now there was *another* thing for Zoe to fix.

"Absolutely not," Zoe said firmly. "You can't quit, Vinnie! We *need* you in the show! I think, with a little more practice, you'll do a great job with your dance routine. I can help you practice, too. Whatever it takes, you're going to shine onstage. I just know it."

For the first time since the paint can catastrophe, Vinnie looked hopeful. "You really think so?" he asked.

"I know so," Zoe promised. "Now, let's get you cleaned up. We can start right away—"

Ring-a-ling!

"Hang on, Vinnie. I'll be right back," Zoe said. She poked her head through the curtain to see who had just entered the pet shop. She could hardly believe her eyes.

"P.S.!" Zoe shrieked. "You're here!"

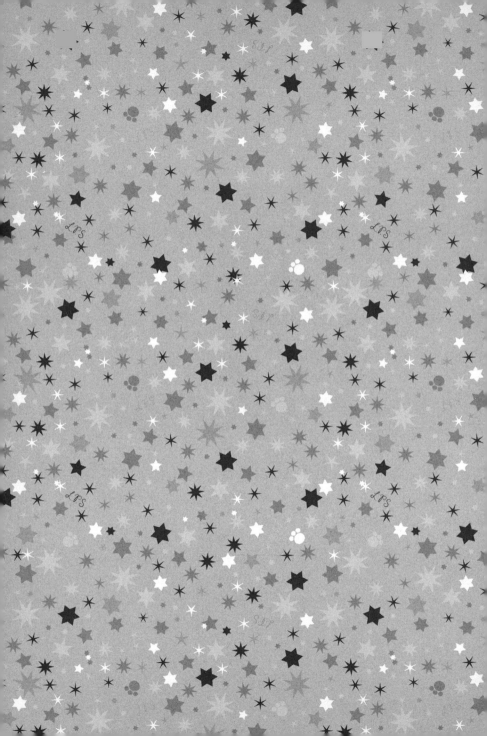

Chapter 4

Philippa trailed P.S., pulling a large suitcase behind her. "Blythe!" she exclaimed.

Zoe zoomed into the front of the Littlest Pet Shop, with Blythe right behind her. Blythe was so surprised to see Philippa that her mouth dropped open. "What are you doing here?" she cried as she rushed forward to give Philippa a hug. "We weren't expecting to see you until Thursday!"

"When P.S. and I got your e-mail, we decided to drive straight to Downtown City—no side stops or detours," Philippa explained with a laugh. "He was already so excited to see you and Zoe—and when he heard about the reunion show, he just wouldn't stop barking. Don't think I'm crazy, Blythe, but sometimes I think that our pets can understand every single word we say!"

Blythe smiled wryly. "I know exactly what you mean," she replied. "Come on in and let me get you a snack. And I bet P.S. would like a little treat, too. How about one of our gourmet pumpkin-and-peanut-butter dog biscuits?"

"He'd love it," Philippa said. She bent down to scratch behind the Maltese's ears. "Judi Jo never let him have treats, but I think every good dog deserves a special snack once in a while."

Blythe reached behind the counter and grabbed two biscuits, one for P.S. and one for Zoe. "I'm sure you two have a lot of catching up to do," she said with a smile.

"You bet we do," Zoe said, but to Philippa's ears, it sounded like *yip-yip-yip-bark!*

"It's so cute how they think they can answer us, isn't it?" Philippa asked Blythe, completely oblivious.

Zoe didn't hear Blythe's response, because she and P.S. were already on their way to the back of the shop. Zoe couldn't wait to tell everyone that P.S. had arrived—and she definitely couldn't wait to spill all the details about the *Terriers and Tiaras* Reunion Show to her famous friend.

"Everybody's back here," Zoe explained as she led P.S. to the Day Camp area. "We've been working constantly to get everything ready for the big show…"

Zoe's voice trailed off as she and P.S. stepped through the curtain. Bubbles drifted by in the air as Penny Ling, Pepper, and Sunil scrambled to clean up the big paint spill, leaving soapy streaks in rainbow colors on the floor.

"And, uh, as you can see, we're still working," Zoe finished.

At the sound of Zoe's voice, Pepper glanced up from her sudsy sponge. "P.S.!" she howled with excitement, and that was all it took for the others to rush over to P.S.

to welcome him back to Downtown City. In an instant, everyone was chattering at once, and the biggest smile Zoe had ever seen appeared on P.S.'s face. It felt like P.S. had never left!

After the pets had a chance to say hello, P.S. turned to Zoe. "Where's everybody else?" he asked.

"As you can see, we had a little, well, mishap this morning," she explained. "Russell, Minka, and Vinnie are washing up now. I'm sure they'll be back in a minute."

"So how's life now that you're off the pageant circuit?" Penny Ling asked eagerly.

"It's amazing!" P.S. told her. "Philippa is such a sweetie—a much better owner than Judi Jo. We sleep in, we eat breakfast together, we take long walks around our neighborhood. Almost every afternoon, Philippa takes me to the dog park so that I can play with my friends back home. Starring on that silly reality show meant living with nonstop drama and stress. I had no idea that life could be so much fun!"

"So you don't miss being on *Terriers and Tiaras*?" asked Pepper.

P.S. tilted his head to the side as he thought about it. "I miss what it *could* have been, I guess," he finally said. "A chance to have fun...to do something different... and most of all, to hang out with my friends. That's why I was so excited when I heard that Zoe was organizing this reunion show. At last, we can put on a show the way it's *supposed* to be."

"Exactly!" Zoe said, nodding her head. "All fun, no drama. That's been our plan from the very beginning."

"No drama…but what happened here?" P.S. said as he gestured to the soapy mess on the floor. "Are you working on some kind of water act for the show?"

"Not exactly," admitted Zoe. "You could call this…technical difficulties."

P.S. nodded knowingly. "That figures," he replied. "I've never been in a show that didn't have some big problems during setup."

"Really? That makes me feel *so* much better," Zoe told him. "I've never done something like this before. To be honest, it's kind of a lot more work than I expected it would be."

P.S. waved his paw in the air. "Don't worry, Zoe. You've got this!" he told her. "When Philippa read Blythe's e-mail to me, I thought, *Only Zoe could come up with an idea* this *great*—and *pull it off!* I mean, how on earth did you even manage to *reach* Sam U.L.?"

Zoe's face wrinkled in confusion. "Reach him?" she repeated. "Well, Blythe sent an e-mail to his owner, of course."

"But they're spending the summer at Camp Tuff Pup," P.S. said. "You know, that doggy wilderness camp in the mountains? They're really roughing it. No cell phones, no television, and definitely no e-mail."

Zoe gulped. "No…e-mail?" she repeated in disbelief.

"Definitely not. In fact, I don't think they even have electricity," P.S. replied.

Just then, a freshly bathed Russell burst into the room. "Guys! Guys!" he yelled. "I've got great news! The manager of the Pawza Hotel just called Blythe, and guess what?

They've already sold more than a hundred tickets to the *Terriers and Tiaras* Reunion Show!"

Zoe gulped. This was great news—or it *should* have been great news—but Zoe felt like she was on the verge of a major freak-out!

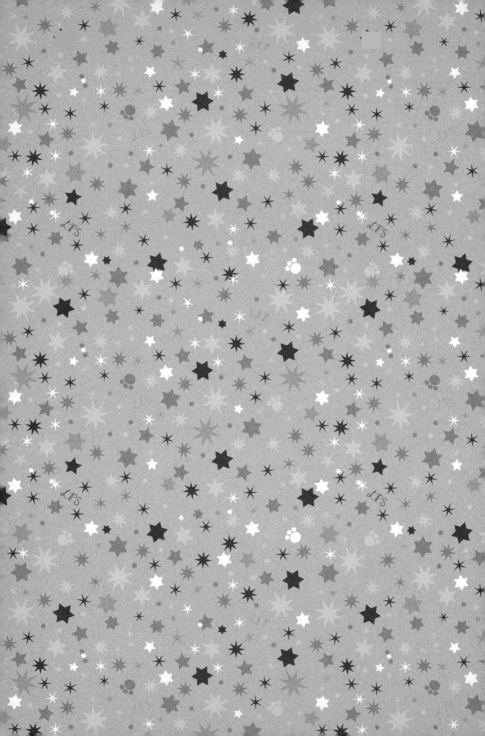

Chapter 5

"*What?*" Zoe shrieked. She started pacing. "This is bad. Really bad. Really, *really* bad."

Russell looked confused. "Bad? What are you talking about? Just think of all the money we've raised for the animal shelter!" he replied.

"No, not *that*," Zoe said. "P.S. just told

me that Sam U.L. is at some doggy camp in the woods, and it doesn't even have electricity, so Tanya probably hasn't even gotten Blythe's e-mail!"

It took a second, but all of a sudden, Russell understood what Zoe was trying to say. "Oh," he said. "*Ohhhhhh. That is bad.*"

"And if Tanya didn't get the e-mail, then she won't know to bring Sam U.L. here for the show!" Zoe howled. "Which means all those posters that Minka painted—all those posters that Blythe hung around Downtown City—are a lie!"

"Hang on, you've gotta fill me in," P.S. spoke up. "What do you mean, a lie?"

"I made Blythe write '*Terriers and Tiaras* Reunion' on every poster," groaned Zoe. "And a bunch of them have a drawing of Sam U.L.! But if Sam U.L. doesn't show up, the audience will get mad! What if they want their money back? What will happen to all the animals at the shelter then?"

Russell and P.S. didn't say anything, but from the look they exchanged, Zoe could tell they were just as worried as she was.

I'm the director, Zoe reminded herself as she took a deep breath. *I'm in charge. And I made this mess, so it's up to me to fix it.*

"Okay, here's what we're going to do," Zoe said, still working on a plan as the words tumbled out of her mouth. "I'll ask Blythe to call that doggy camp, and to e-mail Tanya again, just in case she can get her e-mails after all. Maybe Blythe can send a letter through the mail, too. I mean, there *has* to be a way to reach this place—don't you think? They can't be *completely* cut off from civilization . . . right?"

P.S. opened his mouth to answer, but Zoe kept talking.

"Meanwhile, Minka can make new posters—this time *without* Sam U.L. on them, just in case we can't reach him," she continued. "I mean, we *will* reach him. No matter what it takes. The new posters are, like, a backup plan."

"That's the right attitude," P.S. said encouragingly. "No matter what craziness happens during a show, you've just got to roll with it."

"Yeah!" Russell agreed. "You know what they say—the show must go on!"

Zoe flashed them a grateful smile. "Thanks, guys," she said. "There's no reason to panic. We can handle this!"

Just then, Blythe poked her head through the curtain. "P.S., Philippa says it's time to go," she said. "She wants to get checked in to your room at the Pawza Hotel so you two can rest a little before dinner."

"While I'm there, I'll take a look at the stage and report back," P.S. told Zoe and Russell. "Remember—no stress! This is going to be fun!" Then he followed Blythe to the front of the Littlest Pet Shop.

"I'm so glad P.S. is here," Zoe said to Russell. "We're so lucky to have a real professional in the show."

"A professional what?" Minka asked as she scampered up to them. Minka was still dripping from her bath, but she didn't seem to mind, and as the excited monkey hopped from foot to foot, her short fur dried quickly.

Zoe didn't waste any time telling Minka about everything that had happened—from

P.S.'s surprise early arrival to Russell's report about how many tickets had been sold to the troubling news about Sam U.L.

"I hate to ask this, Minka, but would you make some more posters for me?" Zoe finished. "Blythe was right. I never should've advertised Sam U.L. until I knew for sure that he'd be in the show."

For once, Minka stopped moving. "More posters? I don't know, Zoe," she replied, sounding worried. "I still have to repaint all those stars for the set. What if I run out of time to get it all done?"

"I didn't even think of that," Zoe admitted. "Sorry, Minka. Listen—I'll make the new posters. You can focus on painting the set. Does that sound okay?"

Minka breathed a sigh of relief. "Thanks,

Zoe. That would be great. Feel free to use my art supplies—they're all yours!"

"*Ooh*, I will," Zoe replied, thinking of all the gorgeous art supplies Minka kept at Day Camp. Hundreds of markers, dozens of tubes of glitter, stickers galore...Minka had enough supplies to open her own art store!

"I know I can get the set finished in time for the show now," said Minka.

"And speaking of getting the set finished," Russell spoke up, "let's get back to work!"

Zoe watched Russell and Minka as they hurried over to the set.

"Hey, Zoe!" said a voice from behind her.

Zoe spun around to find Vinnie, who still had a towel draped over his shoulders.

"I'm ready for my first dance lesson!" he announced.

Zoe grimaced. "Oh, Vinnie, I'm sorry," she said. "I have a situation that I've *got* to take care of immediately."

"No problem, Zoe," Vinnie said quickly. "I understand. Maybe later?"

"Definitely," Zoe promised him. "I won't let you down. Let me get these posters ready for Blythe to write on, and then I'll come find you. Make sure you have your dancing shoes on!"

Vinnie pointed at the shiny black shoes on his feet. "Are you kidding? I never take them off!" he said. Sure enough, as Vinnie started walking away, Zoe could hear his shoes going *squish-squish-squish.*

Vinnie didn't wear his shoes in the bath, *did he?* Zoe thought doubtfully. She shook her head as she grabbed a few pieces of poster board and some of Minka's brightest markers.

Zoe stared at the blank poster board. *I'll have to come up with a new poster design,* she thought. *But what should it be?*

Zoe was still trying to figure out the answer to that question when Blythe approached her. "Zoe, I just realized something," Blythe began. "You didn't have a chance to show us your talent! What do you have planned? I want to make sure I design an extra-special costume for our star director."

"Oh, Blythe, that's the *least* of my worries," Zoe replied with a sigh. "I don't know. I was going to do a special dance routine to a Soul Patches song, but right now I've got to make more posters."

"More posters?" Blythe repeated as she

glanced at the art supplies scattered all over the floor. "What about the posters Minka already made?"

Zoe leaned against Blythe—a signal that she wanted a scratch behind her ears. Then she told Blythe all her problems.

"Poor Zoe," Blythe said sympathetically. "It's not easy being in charge, is it?"

"Not really," Zoe admitted. "But I can handle it. I just wish I could draw as well as Minka. I'm worried that my posters will be a disaster compared to hers."

"Hmm. I think what you need to do is put your own unique spin on them," Blythe suggested. "What if the posters focus on fund-raising for the animal shelter instead of the *Terriers and Tiaras* Reunion? Anybody who loves animals will want to buy tickets as soon as they know that the profits go to the shelter."

Zoe brightened right away. "I love that!" she exclaimed. "Then the audience will get a big surprise if—I mean, *when*—the whole cast from *Terriers and Tiaras* goes onstage. Could you write something about the animal shelter at the top of each poster?"

"Sure," Blythe replied. She grabbed a pink marker and wrote HELP THE ANIMALS! in giant bubble letters. Then Blythe added information about the show's date, time, location, and ticket price.

Zoe felt better just seeing some words on the poster board. "Thank you so much, Blythe," she said gratefully. "Now what should I draw on the posters?"

"That's up to you," Blythe said. "I know

you'll figure out something that's as creative and stylish as you are! I'd better get back to the costumes, but if you need help—"

"No, I've got it," Zoe replied quickly. She didn't want to stress Blythe out—designing and sewing *all* the costumes was more than enough work for one person.

After Blythe left, Zoe stared at the posters for a few minutes. *I could draw some animals,* she thought. *But what if they don't look like animals? Maybe I should draw the animal shelter? But that might look kind of boring and sad.*

Zoe sat back as she tried to figure out what she could add to the posters. Then she had a great idea. *Stars!* she thought excitedly. *I* know *I can handle adding some bright, colorful stars—just like the ones Minka and*

Russell are making for the set! Then the posters will match the set, and since we have real stars like P.S. in our show, it all fits together perfectly!

Zoe got right to work, drawing large stars on each poster. At last, she sat back and examined her work. The posters were vibrant and fun, but her design didn't say anything about animals.

And that's when Zoe had her next brilliant idea. *I know* exactly *what these posters need!* she thought excitedly.

Zoe dashed over to Minka's art supplies and searched through them until she found a paint box filled with pretty watercolors. After carefully lining up all the posters in a neat row, Zoe added a few drops of water to each color of paint. Then Zoe took a deep breath, leaped onto the paint palette, and pranced all over each poster!

When Zoe was done, she braced herself before taking a look at the posters. To her delight, they were absolutely perfect! Now, in addition to the colorful stars and Blythe's big letters, a parade of bright paw prints marched across each poster. *I did it*, Zoe thought proudly. It was just the start of tackling the unexpected problems, but successfully dealing with the first one made Zoe feel like she could handle anything.

"Zoe! These posters look *amazing*!" Blythe squealed as she hurried over. "I love what you did with them. Adding paw prints was *genius*!"

As Zoe smiled happily, Blythe took a peek at her phone to check the time. "Tell you what. Let's go hang these posters around town right now. What do you think?"

"But don't you have a ton of work for the costumes?" asked Zoe.

"Yeah...but I can take a short break," Blythe replied. "Come on, it'll be fun—just you and me. We'll take my scooter!"

"Okay! Let's do it!" Zoe said, completely forgetting her promise to help Vinnie as soon as she finished the posters.

Zoe was on her way to the door when Blythe stopped her. "Zoe? I think you're forgetting something," Blythe said with a giggle as she pointed at the floor.

Zoe looked down and gasped. Her paint-covered paws had left a trail of rainbow paw prints all over the floor!

"Don't worry," Blythe told her. "I'll clean

the floor. You go see Mrs. Twombly to wash your toes."

"You got it, Blythe," Zoe replied. She took a step, leaving another paw print on the floor. *Uh-oh*, Zoe thought as she started taking itty-bitty steps on tiptoe. *Who knew show business could be so messy?*

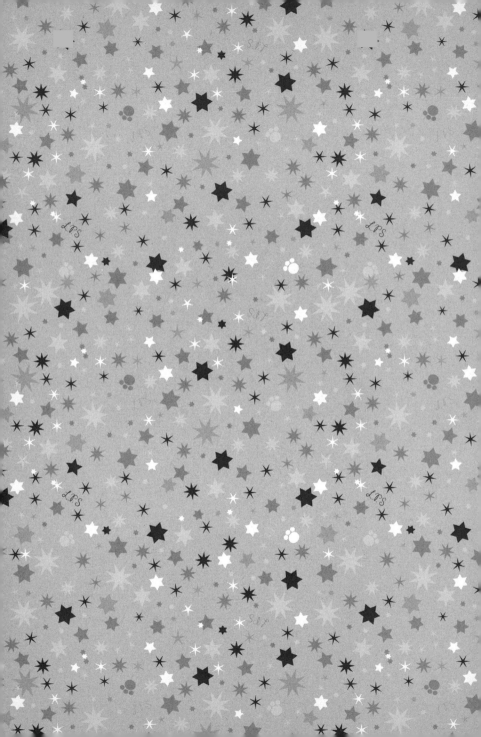

Chapter 6

When Zoe's owners dropped her off for Day Camp the next morning, she went straight to Vinnie. "Vinnie! Yikes! I'm so sorry I didn't have a chance to help you with your routine yesterday," she told him. "Everything got so crazy with P.S. and the new posters and—"

"That's okay, Zoe," he interrupted her.

"You're the director. I get it. You're busier than everybody else."

"But I'll never be too busy for *you*," Zoe replied. "Let's get right to work. Show me the beginning again; then we'll break it down, beat by beat."

As the first notes of the song wafted through the air, Zoe settled in her director's chair to watch Vinnie's routine again. But before Vinnie could even make a move, Zoe felt a tap on her shoulder. She turned around to find Russell standing behind her.

"Got a minute, Zoe?" he asked.

"Well, I'm helping Vinnie with his routine right now," she explained. "What's up?"

"I have a problem with the set pieces," Russell told her.

Oh no! Not another *problem!* Zoe thought

as her heart sank. But all she said to Russell was, "Can it wait until I finish with Vinnie?"

"Sure," he replied. "I'll hang out and watch. I can't do anything else until we figure out how to fix the set."

Zoe shook her head. "No, we don't have any time to waste." Then she turned and called out, "Hold that pose, Vinnie! I have to check on the set, but I'll be right back."

Vinnie froze in place—with his foot high in the air. "Whatever you say, Zoe!" he replied, teetering back and forth.

"No—wait—not *literally*," she replied. "Just remember where you were so we can pick up where we left off as soon as I get back."

"Phew!" Vinnie breathed a sigh of relief as he put his foot on the floor.

Zoe followed Russell to the building area.

Since Zoe had last seen the set, Russell had added several of Minka's colorful stars. A huge grin spread across Zoe's face as she admired their work. "The set looks fantastic!" she cried. "What's the problem?"

"*That's* the problem," Russell replied as he pointed to twelve stars that were scattered around on the ground. "I still have to add the top layer of stars, but I'm afraid of heights!"

"Ohhhh," Zoe said knowingly as she craned her neck to look at the top of the set. It *was* pretty high off the ground. "Well, what about Minka? She's not afraid of heights. I'm sure she'd be happy to help."

Russell glanced around to make sure no one was listening. He leaned close to Zoe, lowered his voice, and whispered, "Would *you* give Minka a hammer?"

"I see your point," Zoe replied. "How about Sunil?"

Russell shook his head. "Forget it. He's so worried that someone will see his magic trick that he's locked himself in a closet with it, and he won't come out!" he said.

"Yikes," Zoe replied. "Well…okay. I guess I can give it a try."

"Great!" Russell exclaimed. "All you have to do is hammer each star to the one below it. It's really very simple!"

That's easy for you to say! Zoe thought anxiously as she stared up at the set. She'd never even used a hammer before!

Russell helped Zoe put on his tool belt. Then he stocked it with his best hammer and dozens of nails. "Ready to go!" he told her as he gestured to a rickety ladder leaning against the set. "When you get to the top of the ladder, I'll hoist a star up with the pulley. They don't weigh much, so it should only take a couple of nails to attach each one."

Zoe gulped. "Any advice?" she asked.

Russell nodded his head. "Yes," he replied seriously. "Don't look down! And definitely don't hammer your paw. That really hurts!"

That's when Zoe noticed the giant bandages on Russell's paws. "Poor Russell! Are you okay?" she exclaimed.

"I will be," he replied. "In fact, I'm doing better already—now that you're going to finish building the set."

Zoe smiled—or tried to smile, at least. "Okay," she said as she took a deep breath. "Here we go!"

Rung by rung, an inch at a time, Zoe

crawled up the ladder. "This isn't so bad," she called down to Russell.

"You're a natural up there," Russell told her.

"Maybe my talent for the show could be ladder climbing," she joked.

"What? You mean *you* don't have a talent planned?" he asked in surprise.

"I—well—you know—" Zoe stammered. "It's been so busy—"

"But, Zoe! You've got to have a talent!" Russell exclaimed. "You were on *Terriers and Tiaras*! You're one of the *stars*!"

"Don't worry, Russell. I'll figure it out," she said. "I'll do some sort of dance. I'll start practicing as soon as—*whoa!*"

"What? What's wrong?" Russell cried anxiously. "Are you okay up there?"

"Yes, I'm fine—just surprised!" Zoe replied. "I can't believe I reached the top already!"

"Let's get you a star!" Russell said as he began pulling on a rope to hoist one of the stars up to Zoe. Soon it was swinging beside her.

"What do I do now?" Zoe called to him.

"Just push it next to one of the stars that's already attached to the set. Then start hammering!" Russell explained.

That sounds simple enough, Zoe thought. There was just one problem: How on earth could she manage to hold on to the star, the ladder, the hammer, and the nail all at the same time?

Let's see...grab the ladder with my back paws, push the star with my nose, hammer in one front paw and nails in the other, Zoe decided. *Yes! That should work.*

"Zoe? You okay up there?" Russell asked in a worried voice as Zoe twisted and turned on the top of the ladder.

"Never better!" Zoe replied, sounding more confident than she felt. She reached out as far as she could for the star. *Almost... got... it,* she thought, filled with determination. Suddenly, Zoe felt the ladder shift beneath her!

"Whoa-whoa-whoa-*whoa*!" she cried as the ladder wobbled back and forth.

As Zoe scrambled to grab hold of the ladder, the nails flew out of her paw and hit the floor. *Ping! Ping! Ping! Ping!* Russell needed to use some fancy footwork to jump out of the way!

"Are you okay?" Zoe and Russell shouted at the same time.

"Don't worry about me; I'm fine," Russell said right away. "How are *you*?"

"Yes…I'm…fine," Zoe replied, taking several deep breaths to calm her pounding heart. "I'm so glad you didn't get hurt. I've heard of a hailstorm, but a *nailstorm*? That's dangerous!" she exclaimed. "I think we're going to need somebody to help hold the ladder."

"I'd do it, but my paws are tied," Russell told Zoe. "See?" He held up his paws to show her how he'd twisted the pulley's rope through them.

"I guess we'll just have to call for help and hope someone hears us," Zoe said.

"Did somebody say help?" a new voice spoke up.

Zoe peered down at the floor and got a wonderful surprise: Shea Butter had arrived!

"Hooray! You're here!" Zoe cried with such excitement that she made the ladder wobble again.

The tiny Yorkie stared up at Zoe with a look of alarm on her face. Shea Butter could tell right away what she needed to do. She raced over to the ladder and held it firmly against the wall. And that was all Zoe needed to start hammering away! Soon she was hammering the very last nail into the very last star.

The instant she was done, Zoe scrambled down the ladder to give Shea Butter a proper welcome. Of all the pups on *Terriers and Tiaras*, Shea Butter was the most pampered. Her owner, Cindeanna, was completely devoted to Shea Butter. Cinde-anna would do just about anything to spoil her precious pet! But sometimes what Shea Butter wanted most of all was the chance to be a regular dog instead of a pampered show dog who was carried everywhere on a velvet pillow. It wasn't until Shea Butter met Zoe that she found a way to show Cinde-anna how she really felt about dog shows. Ever since then, Shea Butter's life had been much more normal.

"Come on, let's get you fitted for your costume," Zoe told Shea Butter. "And I just know Blythe would love to say hello!"

On the way to Blythe's sewing center, Zoe saw Vinnie—still standing right where she'd left him, wearing his shiny black danc-ing shoes.

"Oh no! Vinnie, I'm sorry," Zoe said in a

rush. "Finishing up the set took a *lot* longer than I thought it would, and now Shea Butter's here, and—"

"Don't worry about it, Zoe," Vinnie said. "I practiced by myself while you were busy. I think I'm doing better. A lot better!"

"You are?" Zoe yipped happily. "That's fantastic, Vinnie! In that case, I'm just going to run over to see if Blythe needs any help designing a costume for Shea Butter."

Vinnie's face fell. "I was hoping—"

"Later on, you show me what you've got, okay?" Zoe said brightly. "Can't wait to see your new routine!"

When Zoe and Shea Butter reached Blythe, they discovered that Cindeanna had beaten them to it.

"There you are, sweetie pie," Cindeanna cooed as she scooped Shea Butter into her arms. "Come along. Mommy's made arrangements for you to have some deluxe spa treatments after that *exhausting* drive!"

As soon as Cindeanna and Shea Butter left, Blythe let out a frustrated sigh.

"What's wrong?" asked Zoe.

"Let's just say that Cindeanna has some big ideas for Shea Butter's costume," Blythe said, gritting her teeth. "Ruffles...ribbons... sequins...and all of it sewed by hand!"

"But, Blythe, Shea Butter doesn't care about that stuff," Zoe told her.

"I know...but her owner does," Blythe replied. "Cindeanna went to a lot of trouble to bring Shea Butter here for the show. Making a spectacular costume for Shea Butter seems like the least I can do. I just wish I knew how to find the time to get everything done!"

And I wish I knew how to take some of the stress away, Zoe thought anxiously. Then she realized exactly what she could do. "Actually, Blythe, I was thinking about it, and I think I should make my own costume for the show."

Blythe's eyes grew wide. "Oh, Zoe, you don't have to do that—"

"No, I *want* to," Zoe said quickly before Blythe could argue. "Russell and I were just talking about my, um, act for the show, and now that I think about it, I should probably make some changes to my costume plans, too."

After all, Zoe thought, *if I haven't even figured out exactly what I want to do in the show, there's no reason to stick to my original costume idea.*

"Well...if you're sure..." Blythe said, but she didn't sound convinced.

"I am," Zoe said firmly. Then she gave Blythe her biggest smile to prove it.

"Thanks, Zoe." Blythe finally gave in. "And if you need any help…"

Zoe waved her paw in the air. "Don't worry. I'll be fine," she said. Inside, though, Zoe wasn't so sure. The show was getting closer and closer, but her to-do list was getting longer and longer. *Isn't it supposed to be the other way around?* she wondered.

Chapter 7

Two days before the show, Zoe called a meeting of the entire cast and crew—Russell, Minka, Blythe, Penny Ling, Pepper, Sunil, Vinnie—and, of course, P.S. and Shea Butter. The Day Camp area of the Littlest Pet Shop was more crowded than usual—but it was also cozier than usual.

On an ordinary day, Zoe would've liked to curl up and take a little nap, but this was no time for sleeping!

"Blythe, would you please open that window?" Zoe asked. "It's a little warm in here."

"Sure," Blythe replied as she pushed open the window, scattering a flock of pigeons that had perched there. "Sorry, pigeons," Blythe told them. From the way they immediately landed on the windowsill again, the birds didn't seem to mind the interruption.

"We're so close, everybody," Zoe told her friends. "And it never would've been possible without all your hard work!"

Zoe started clapping for her pals, and soon everyone else joined in, too.

"There's still a lot to do, though," Zoe continued when the group was quiet again.

"Let's start by going over the schedule. Today, all the performers will have their final fittings with Blythe to make sure their costumes are just right. Then, tomorrow, we'll transport the set over to the Pawza Hotel and have a big dress rehearsal to make sure everything goes according to plan."

"Any news about Sam U.L.?" asked P.S.

Zoe shook her head sadly. "Not yet," she admitted. "We've done everything—sent letters, sent e-mails, sent texts. Blythe even left two messages at Camp Tuff Pup headquarters. At this point, I'd do anything to reach Sam U.L. and Tanya. I'd even try sending a message with a carrier pigeon!"

"There's still a chance Tanya got my messages, Zoe," Blythe pointed out. "After all, if it's hard to get messages *to* her, it's probably just as hard to get messages *from* her."

Zoe perked right up. "I hadn't thought of it like that before," she said. "Maybe they're on their way here right now."

"There's always hope," Blythe replied. Then she stood up. "Okay, everybody, let's try on your costumes and see how they fit!"

"Minka and I will start packing up the set and props so they don't get damaged on the way over to the Pawza," Russell said.

"Great," Zoe said as she felt a shiver of excitement. Now more than ever the *Terriers and Tiaras* Reunion Show seemed like it was really happening!

And best of all, I finally *have a little time to figure out my own act and costume,* Zoe thought with relief. Yes, it was last minute. Yes, there was still a lot of work ahead of her. But Zoe knew that if she didn't finalize her talent today, she wouldn't have enough time to practice before the show.

Music, Zoe thought. *First, I'll have to pick out a song.* She went over to the closet where Mrs. Twombly stored the portable CD player and the pets' favorite CDs. To Zoe's surprise, she found Vinnie in there, putting all the CDs in alphabetical order.

"Vinnie, what are you doing here?" Zoe asked him. "Aren't you going to try on your costume for Blythe?"

"Oh...about that..." Vinnie replied. "I've been thinking about it, and, well, I've decided I'm not going to be in the show."

"You're not?" Zoe exclaimed. "What are you talking about?"

"I thought I could be the number one fan in the audience," he explained. "I'm just...not that good at dancing, you know? But I *am* pretty great at clapping!"

A pang of guilt hit Zoe. "You can't drop out now," she told him. "Come on—show me your best moves. And if you need any extra help, I'm here for you."

"But—you've been so busy," Vinnie said. "Don't you have, like, a million billion other, more important things to do?"

Zoe pushed thoughts of her own talent and costume out of her mind. "No, I don't," she replied—and she meant it, too. "Get your music, and let's get started!"

Vinnie's face lit up like the fireworks at the Downtown City Founder's Day Celebration. "Thanks, Zoe! You're the best!" he cried.

Zoe plunked right down on the floor of the closet to watch. In that moment, Vinnie didn't need a stage or a costume, and she didn't need her fancy director's chair or her clipboard. All that mattered were the moves and the music.

"So I'm going to start off like this," Vinnie said, striking a pose. "Then go left-left-left, right-right-right...a big spin...then a triple twirl..."

Zoe didn't say anything while she watched Vinnie perform his routine. She could tell that he'd changed it a lot, but it still wasn't quite right. As soon as he finished dancing, Vinnie looked at Zoe with hope in his eyes.

"Much better," she told him. "I can tell how hard you've been working."

"Really?" Vinnie replied. "I don't know. I still feel like something's missing."

Zoe tapped her paw thoughtfully. "I think it could be a little tighter," she replied. "And maybe you should save the triple turn for the very end."

"Oh, like a big-finish, grand-finale kind of thing?" Vinnie asked, nodding his head. "Yeah! That would look great!"

"Exactly! I think dance routines look really good when they build up to a big ending," Zoe told him. "I also had a new idea for the beginning. Watch this."

Zoe hopped up and did a few quick moves, followed by a low kick.

"Wow! That was great!" Vinnie exclaimed.

"Now we'll do it together," she encouraged him. "And a one, and a two, and a *three*!"

Vinnie took a deep breath and tried to copy Zoe's moves exactly.

"Wow, Vinnie! You're a fast learner!" she told him. Her eyes twinkled. "So tell me… have you ever done a backflip before?"

"A backflip? Me?" Vinnie asked. He shook his head. "I'm willing to try, though. Maybe *that's* what my dance has been missing."

"I have an idea for a big finish—a *really* big finish," Zoe said. "And with a little practice, I know that you'll nail it!"

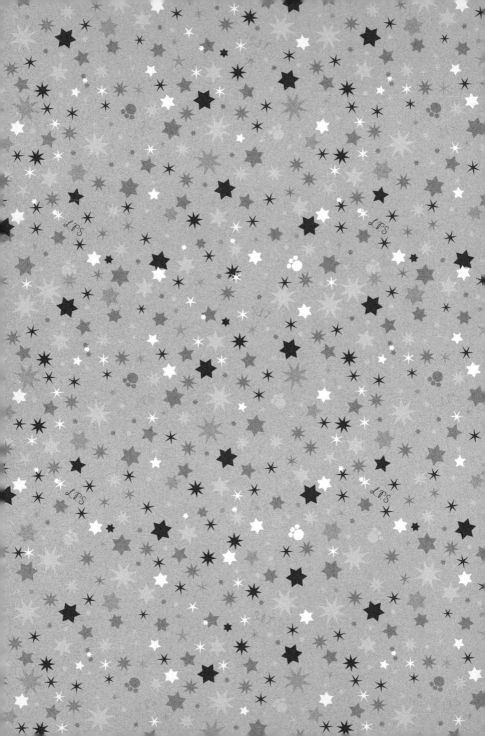

Chapter 8

The next evening, Zoe could hardly believe that it was time for the dress rehearsal! She and Vinnie had spent the entire morning putting the finishing touches on his routine. Then Zoe, Blythe, and Blythe's dad, Roger, had brought all the props and set pieces over to the Pawza Hotel. The new lounge, with its glittering lights, elegant seats, and highly polished stage, was so glamorous that it took Zoe's breath away.

When it was time for the dress rehearsal, Mrs. Twombly drove the pets over to the Pawza Hotel. Mrs. Twombly, Cindeanna, Philippa, and the manager of the Pawza Hotel all wanted to stay and watch the dress rehearsal. It wasn't easy, but Blythe eventually convinced them to wait for the real show.

"The pets and I have some big surprises planned," she explained. "And we wouldn't want to ruin them."

When Blythe and the pets were finally alone, Zoe took charge. "Okay, first things first," she announced. "Let's have everybody line up in this order: P.S., Penny Ling, Shea Butter, Pepper, Sunil, then me, and, finally, Vinnie."

When everyone was assembled, Zoe took a long look at them. "Yes. Perfect," she said. "Don't forget to leave a little room after Pepper. That's where Sam U.L. will stand." *I hope*, Zoe thought—but she kept it to herself.

"Okay," Zoe continued. "So first up, we'll have everybody parade onto the stage in this order, kind of like a fashion show. Then we'll start the acts. First is P.S.'s hoop jumping, then Penny Ling's ribbon dance, Shea Butter's tumbling, Pepper's mime routine, followed by whatever Sam U.L. wants to perform. Then we'll have Sunil's magic trick. My act will be next...and Vinnie will finish the show. And then we'll all take a bow together at the very end."

Blythe's eyes twinkled. "Better be prepared for at least two curtain calls," she said. "I think the crowd is going to go wild!"

"I sure hope so," replied Zoe. Then she turned back to the group. "Now, Blythe will be introducing each act, and Minka will cue the music. Russell, of course, will be in charge of the lighting and the curtain. So let's have everybody get backstage and run through the whole show!"

As the pets climbed the stage, Zoe stayed behind.

"Hey, Zoe," Vinnie called. "Aren't you coming with us?"

Zoe shook her head. "I'm going to watch from out here," she explained. "That way, I can give notes if anything's not working. But don't worry—I'll be backstage with everyone else tomorrow night."

When all the pets were assembled back-stage, Zoe called, "Russell—lights out!"

The entire lounge was plunged into darkness. In the silence, Zoe felt a thrill stir inside her as she imagined this moment tomorrow night when she would be behind the curtain with the rest of the performers, and every seat in the audience would be filled.

Then, slowly, the lights began to brighten. The curtain opened, revealing the set. Under the shining spotlights, all the shimmering stars were even more gorgeous than Zoe had imagined they would be!

Blythe stepped up to the microphone. "Ladies and gentlemen, boys and girls, and pets of all kinds—welcome to the first-ever *Terriers and Tiaras* Reunion Show!" she announced.

On Blythe's cue, all the pets marched

onto the stage with their heads held high. In their fabulous costumes, they were even more impressive than the star-studded set!

Zoe settled into her seat to watch each act. P.S.'s flashy hoop jumping was the perfect way to start the show, and Shea Butter's high-energy tumbling routine made everyone clap and cheer. But when it was Sunil's turn, he walked onto the stage wearing his magician costume—and just stood there.

"Sunil?" Zoe called from the audience. "Aren't you going to do your magic trick?"

He shook his head. "Not until tomorrow," he replied. "I don't want to spoil it."

Zoe tried not to sigh. "Okay, if you insist," she said. "So let's move on to Vinnie."

The little gecko's head peeked out from the wings. "But I thought you're going after Sunil," he replied.

Zoe frowned. Technically, Vinnie was correct. The only problem was that Zoe *still* didn't have an act ready to perform, but she didn't want anyone to know, so she decided to follow Sunil's lead. "I'm keeping it a surprise," she said quickly. "You'll just have to wait until tomorrow."

"Oh, okay." Vinnie shrugged as he walked onto the stage. Then he showed off his new and improved dance routine. Zoe smiled proudly as she watched Vinnie dance. He was definitely doing better!

At the end of the rehearsal, Zoe was full of praise for all the pets. Somehow, against the odds, they were going to pull it off! *And I still have the whole night to figure out my routine and make my costume,* Zoe thought as she stifled a yawn. There was just one problem: She needed to be at the Littlest Pet Shop, with access to all the music and Blythe's sewing supplies. Zoe trotted up to her friend to ask for some help.

"Blythe," Zoe said in a low voice, "you've got to convince my owners to let me sleep over at the Littlest Pet Shop tonight."

Blythe looked surprised. "But, Zoe, you should get a good night's sleep," she replied. "Tomorrow is such a big day. Won't you rest better at home, in your own cozy bed?"

"Definitely not!" Zoe said. "I've got to go over the schedule one last time. And make sure everything's ready. And pack all the stage makeup. And…a bunch of other things, too. I won't get a wink of sleep at home if I'm constantly worrying that I forgot to do something! Plus, if—I mean, *when*—Sam U.L. and Tanya arrive, I want to be there to meet them."

"Okay," Blythe finally agreed, though she didn't sound convinced. "I'll call your owners as soon as we get back to the Littlest Pet Shop."

"Thanks, Blythe!" Zoe said gratefully. "You're the best!"

It took a couple of hours to put away all the props and costumes and get everybody back to the Littlest Pet Shop. By the time the last pet had been picked up and Mrs. Twombly was ready to lock up, it was already past Zoe's bedtime—and she was feeling sleepier than ever. The only sound in the empty shop was the *click-click-click* of Zoe's paws as she stepped across the smooth floor.

It won't take too long to figure out my act, she tried to tell herself as she slipped into the room where Blythe had made all the costumes. *I just have to pick out a song . . . work on my dance moves . . . find some fabric . . . make a costume . . .*

Zoe rubbed a paw across her eyes as she yawned again.

This fabric looks nice, she thought as she touched a beautiful bolt of velvet on the floor near Blythe's sewing machine. *It's so soft. Maybe I'll just sit here for a minute . . . take a tiny little rest to get my energy up . . . and then I'll . . .*

But Zoe never even had a chance to finish her thought. As soon as she laid her head on the cozy, cushiony velvet, she fell fast asleep.

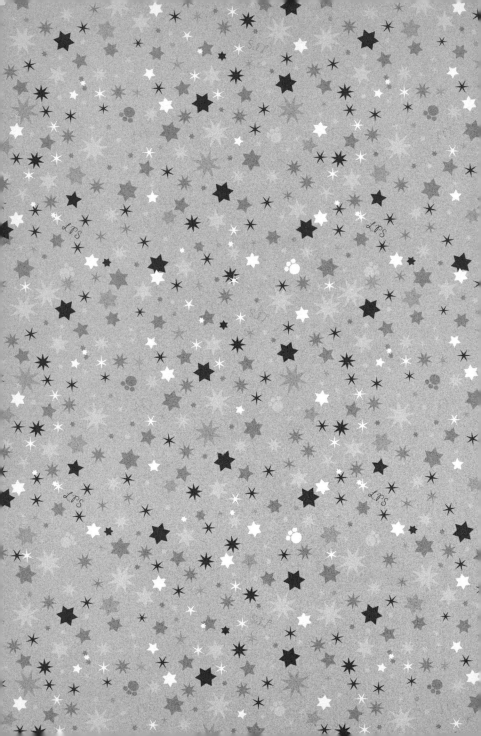

Chapter 9

Hours later, Zoe stretched and smiled, still fast asleep. In Zoe's dream, her costume was gorgeous and her performance was perfect. The entire show was an enormous success! No wonder the crowd was calling her name: "Zoe! Zoe! Zoe!" She wanted to savor this moment forever.

"Zoe! Zoe! Wake up!"

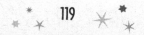

Someone was shaking her shoulders.

Zoe opened her eyes and blinked. She looked up to see all her closest friends gathered around: Blythe, Minka, Pepper, Penny Ling, Sunil, Vinnie, and Russell. It only took a second for Zoe to realize that she wasn't onstage at all; she was wrapped up in Blythe's velvet fabric in the back of the Littlest Pet Shop. That meant that the show hadn't happened yet. She'd been dreaming.

"Why did you sleep in the workshop?" Blythe asked in concern. "I thought you'd use one of the pet beds."

Why did *I sleep in the workshop?* Zoe wondered. *I was making my costume...wait...did I make my costume?*

Then it all came flooding back: how terribly tired she was, how cozy the velvet fabric was, how it seemed like a good idea to rest for just a minute or two. Zoe gasped in horror. She'd fallen asleep before choreographing her dance routine and making her costume...and from the look of the bright sunshine flooding the room, she'd slept through the whole night and half the day!

"Oh no!" Zoe howled. "The show is *today*—and I'm not ready!"

"Not ready?" Russell asked. "But, Zoe, you've been working like a dog for days and days."

Zoe paced frantically. "Everything's ruined—everything!" she sobbed. "Sam U.L. never showed up, and now I can't be in the show, either!"

"What are you talking about?" Blythe asked, confused. "Of *course* you'll be in the show, Zoe! You've worked so hard—"

Zoe shook her head. "But I don't have a talent to perform," she explained miserably. "I never figured out what to do onstage. There was always something more important to take care of. I don't even have a costume to wear!"

At last, Zoe's big secret was out. But hearing herself say the words just made her start howling louder.

"No Sam U.L. No Zoe. How can we call it a *Terriers and Tiaras* Reunion Show if half the cast is missing?" Zoe continued. "The whole show is falling apart…and it's all my fault!"

Blythe sat back and looked at Zoe thoughtfully. "Yes…I guess it *is* your fault," she said in a voice that made everyone turn to look at her. "If you hadn't had such a wonderful idea—"

"If you hadn't e-mailed my owner," Shea Butter spoke up.

"If you hadn't drawn the new posters," added Minka.

"And finished building the set," Russell said.

"And told me to focus on making everyone else's costumes instead of yours," continued Blythe.

"And helped me rehearse," Penny Ling said while Pepper nodded.

"And taught me how to dance," said Vinnie.

"There wouldn't be a show at all," Blythe finished. "Don't you see, Zoe? If you're not completely ready to perform in the show, it's only because you've been working so hard to help everybody else."

Zoe tried to smile, but it looked all

wobbly. "It's very sweet of you to say that, Blythe, but the truth is, I couldn't pull it off," she said. "I thought I could—I really, really wanted to—but it was just too much for me."

"No way, Zoe," Blythe said firmly. "You've worked way too hard to give up now! We still have an hour before we need to be at the Pawza Hotel. That's plenty of time for me to whip up a quick costume for you. It might not be super fancy, but it will definitely be beautiful."

"But, Blythe, I don't even *need* a costume," Zoe said. "I don't have an act, remember?"

"Yes, you do," Vinnie announced. He held out a hand to Zoe. "You'll be dancing with *me* tonight."

"With you?" Zoe asked. "Like...a pas de deux?"

Vinnie nodded enthusiastically. "Yeah! I bet you know the routine by heart already. You helped me practice it for *hours* and *hours*. You pretty much choreographed the whole thing!"

"Backflips *are* one of my specialties," Zoe said. "But I don't want to barge in on your act. That wouldn't be fair."

"What wouldn't be fair is if you missed the chance to perform tonight," Vinnie said. "Come on, Zoe! Let's go practice one last time."

Blythe scrambled to her feet. "If you're dancing with Vinnie, I know just what to make for your costume!" she cried excitedly as she dashed over to the sewing machine. "Something compatible, but not *too* matchy-matchy...and of course, a little extra flair to showcase all your big moves.

A costume that will look as great as your dance!"

Hope radiated through Zoe's heart. Maybe, just maybe, everything was going to work out after all!

"Thank you, everyone!" she cried. "I really do have the best friends ever!"

"You can thank us later," Blythe teased her with a big smile. "But right now, you'd better start practicing!"

Zoe and Vinnie spent the next hour changing his solo dance into a routine that was perfect for two. With a few extra twirls and a new and even bigger finish, Zoe even started to feel like she was a real part of the routine and not just an afterthought. All the while, Blythe's sewing machine went *clackity-clackity-clack* as she furiously sewed a costume for Zoe to wear. It almost sounded like the machine was keeping time with the music.

"Finished!" Blythe finally cried. "Time to try it on!"

"I'm on my way!" Zoe exclaimed as she hurried over.

As Blythe helped Zoe into her beautiful new costume, Zoe closed her eyes. She could hardly wait to see her reflection in the mirror.

"Well?" Blythe asked. "What do you think?"

Zoe took a step toward the mirror and opened her eyes. Then she looked over at Blythe and held her paw over her heart. "Oh, Blythe," she whispered. "It's perfect! Thank you, thank you, *thank you!*"

The bright red skirt Blythe had whipped up for Zoe had an extra layer of flouncy ruffles, plus dozens of sequins scattered around it. Matching ribbon roses for Zoe to wear behind her ears added the perfect finishing touch. Zoe did a little twirl to watch the skirt flare out as she moved. She had never felt prettier!

Just then, Mrs. Twombly poked her head into Day Camp. "Oh, Zoe, don't you look adorable!" she cooed. "Blythe, you've truly outdone yourself putting this show together. I know all the pets would thank you if they could!"

Blythe and Zoe exchanged a secret smile. Of course, Mrs. Twombly would never understand just how hard all the pets had worked, too—and there was no way for Blythe to explain it.

"Anyway, I was just popping in to see if everyone was ready," Mrs. Twombly continued. "The show starts in a little over an hour, you know?"

Zoe's heart started pounding. "An hour!" she exclaimed. "Does that mean what I think it means?"

Blythe's eyes twinkled. "It sure does," she replied. "Time to load up the van and head over to the Pawza Hotel. It's *showtime!*"

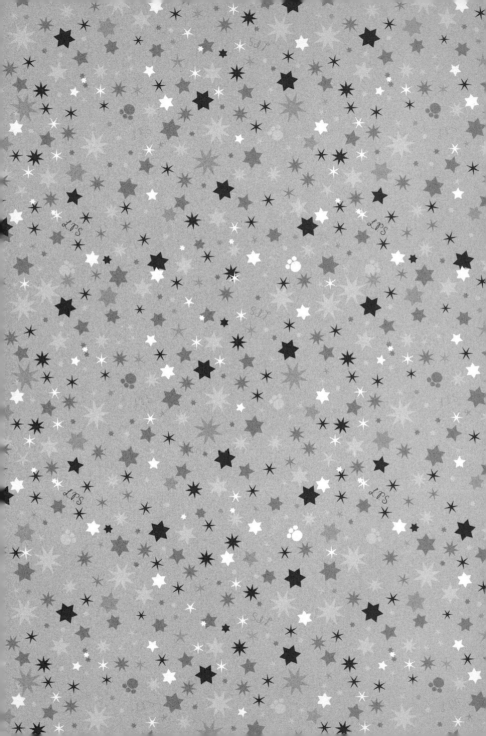

Chapter 10

Standing behind the heavy velvet curtain onstage at the Pawza Hotel, Zoe could hear dozens—maybe even hundreds—of muffled voices chatting and laughing as the audience members found their seats. In just a few more moments, Russell would raise the curtain, and the show would begin!

Zoe hurried down the line of her friends,

making sure everyone was in the proper position. When she came to the gap behind Pepper, though, she paused. *I guess it's time to face the truth*, Zoe thought sadly. *Sam U.L. didn't make it after all.* Zoe had never given up hope that somehow a miracle would happen just in time for Sam U.L. to join the show. But as Blythe adjusted the microphone and Russell got ready to raise the curtain, Zoe knew they were out of time.

"It's okay, Sunil," Zoe said in a low voice. "You can move forward. Sam U.L. isn't coming."

"Says who?" someone asked.

Zoe spun around to see Sam U.L.—the one and only!—standing right behind her! Her mouth dropped open in shock.

"But—what—how—why—" Zoe sputtered.

"I thought—you never—Sam U.L.! You made it! You're here!"

The shaggy brown Brussels griffon chuckled as Zoe gave him a big hug. "You didn't really think I'd miss the first-ever *Terriers and Tiaras* Reunion, did you, Zoe?" he asked.

"P.S. told us that you were completely unreachable," Zoe explained. "I didn't know if you even got our messages."

Sam U.L. grew serious. "I almost didn't," he replied. "P.S. was right. At Camp Tuff Pup, we're completely cut off from e-mail, phone—everything."

"So how *did* you find out about the show?" Zoe asked, confused.

"You'll never believe it," Sam U.L. began. "Yesterday afternoon, a flock of pigeons flew up to the camp to tell me about the show. They'd heard all about it from their cousins who live right here in Downtown City!"

Suddenly, Zoe remembered the flock of pigeons that were perched on the window-sill of the Littlest Pet Shop when she'd held a meeting for the cast and crew. *I made a joke about carrier pigeons,* she thought with a grin, *but I never expected them to follow through!* She'd have to remember to ask Blythe to give the pigeons some birdseed when they got back to the Littlest Pet Shop. Those birds had saved the show!

"Tanya and I drove all night long to get here," Sam U.L. continued. "It gave me plenty of time to work on my talent. I think the crowd will go wild when they see my Barking Boot Camp routine!"

"I *know* they will!" Zoe declared.

Just then, Blythe appeared. She grinned when she saw Sam U.L. "You made it!" Blythe whispered happily as she patted his head. She turned to the rest of the pets. "Everybody ready? The lights will dim in one minute. At that moment, I'll welcome the audience, and the curtain will open. Do you all remember what to do?"

The pets nodded in response.

"Break a leg, everybody!" Blythe told them.

Zoe quickly showed Sam U.L. where to stand. "You'll follow Pepper, first in the parade, then for your talent," she explained in a rush. "I wish we had time to practice, but—"

"Don't worry, Zoe," Sam U.L. interrupted her with a grin. "I'm a professional!"

Zoe grinned back as she took her place

in line. The murmurs of the audience grew silent, all at once. *The lights*, Zoe realized, remembering this moment from when she'd been sitting in the audience for the dress rehearsal. *Russell must have dimmed them— and now everybody knows that the show is about to begin.*

Zoe heard Blythe's voice echo over the speakers. "Ladies and gentlemen, boys and girls, pets of all kinds—welcome to the *Terriers and Tiaras* Reunion Show!" Blythe announced into the microphone, just like she had during the dress rehearsal.

With a sudden *whoosh*, the curtain opened. Zoe stood straighter. This was it: their cue. P.S. didn't miss a beat as he strode onto the stage, followed by Penny Ling, Shea Butter, Pepper, Sam U.L., and Sunil.

Then it was Zoe's turn. She took a deep breath, put one paw in front of the other...

And marched onto the stage!

The dazzling lights were so bright that Zoe could hardly see all the people in the audience, but from their noisy cheers, she could tell that it was a packed house. She smiled bigger with every step she took. This was it—the moment she'd been dreaming of all week—and Zoe could already tell that she never wanted it to end!

At the end of the Pet Parade, Zoe found herself backstage once more. There wasn't enough room for everybody in the wings, but if Zoe scrunched against the wall, there was just enough space for her to watch each performance without being seen by the audience. Zoe's heart swelled with pride as she watched her friends perform. All their hard work and dedication made the acts seem better than ever before! From the beauty of Penny Ling's swirling ribbon to the silliness of Pepper's mime routine, each act was unique and wonderful in its own way...just like Zoe's pals.

Sam U.L. marched onto the stage and wowed the crowd with his tough-guy boot camp drills. Zoe found herself tapping her paw along to the beat—and so did the audience, which told Zoe that everyone watching the show was having as much fun as she was. *This is why it was so important for Sam U.L. to be here,* Zoe thought happily. *It really wouldn't have been the same without him.*

When Sunil took the stage for his magic trick, Zoe realized how glad she was that he had insisted on keeping it a secret—because she was more surprised than anyone when he somehow made paw-print-shaped confetti rain down on the entire audience!

As Sunil took a bow, Vinnie joined Zoe in the wings. That could only mean one thing: Their pas de deux was next!

"Ready, Zoe?" he whispered.

"Ready, Vinnie!" she replied.

When the first notes of their song drifted through the air, Zoe and Vinnie pranced onto the stage. From the loud *tappity-tappity-tappity-tap* of their special dance shoes, Zoe could tell that she and Vinnie were dancing in perfect unison, doing all the same moves at the exact same time. Zoe stepped back so that Vinnie could show off the fancy footwork they'd practiced. She held her breath as she watched him dance—but Vinnie didn't miss a beat! The crowd was cheering as he stepped back for Zoe's mini solo.

With the spotlight—and all eyes—on her, Zoe started dancing with her heart and soul. The moves she'd practiced with Vinnie felt as natural and easy as strolling through Downtown City Park on a sunny day. A double dip, a triple twirl, the feel of her ruffly skirt fluttering with every move she made...Zoe was loving it! And so was the audience. Out of the corner of her eye, Zoe could see that everyone out there had jumped to their feet and was clapping along with the music. That's when she realized that the real glory of performing didn't come from starring in the spotlight. It came from bringing joy to everyone watching the show.

Right on cue, Vinnie moved next to Zoe for their big finish. They glanced at each other and exchanged a quick nod before—

"One..." Zoe whispered.

"Two..." Vinnie whispered back.

"Three!" they shouted together.

With a tremendous leap into the air, both Zoe and Vinnie pulled off two perfect backflips—at the exact same time! The crowd went wild. It was the perfect ending to the perfect show.

"I think we figured out what my routine was missing, Zoe," Vinnie said.

"What's that?" Zoe asked as she tried to catch her breath.

"You!" he replied.

As the rest of the pets filed onto the stage for the curtain call, Zoe felt a sudden pang of sadness. *I don't want it to end,* she thought. The thunderous applause...the gorgeous costumes...the dazzling lights... putting on the show had been a *ton* of work and worry, but Zoe wouldn't have changed a thing about it.

After the performers took their bow, Minka, Russell, and Blythe joined them onstage to get some credit for all the fine work they'd done behind the scenes. Then something completely unexpected happened. With a wave and a whistle, Blythe beckoned to someone offstage. Zoe's ears perked up. This was *not* something they had rehearsed...and from the reactions of the other pets onstage with her, Zoe could tell they were just as confused as she was.

Everyone watched in surprise as workers from the animal shelter walked onto the stage. Each one escorted an animal who

Zoe had never seen before: cute cats, roly-poly pups—even a bunny and some birds. The audience seemed to know that something special was about to happen. The cheers and claps quieted as everyone sat down again, eager to see what would happen next.

Blythe stepped over to the microphone once more. "Friends, I have a big announcement to make!" she said with an enormous smile on her face. "All the profits from the ticket sales for tonight's show have been donated to the Downtown City Animal Shelter. And I thought you should see for yourselves just what that means. Tonight, all these pets—every last one of them—have had their food and medical care paid for. That means they're ready to be adopted, thanks to all of you!"

In an instant, the audience members were on their feet again, clapping, cheering, and screaming as loud as they could! The animals onstage joined in, too, barking and meowing and stomping their paws. There was pandemonium in the Pawza Hotel!

When the crowd finally quieted again, Blythe continued. "So if anyone in the audience is looking for a furry friend to join your family, we have adoption applications for you to fill out, and some very special pets who'd love to meet you. Thank you all for your support, and have a great night!"

From center stage, Zoe watched as members of the audience hurried forward to get adoption applications and meet the animals from the shelter.

Blythe crossed the stage and knelt beside Zoe. "This is all thanks to you, you know," she said in a low voice as she adjusted Zoe's ribbon roses. "From putting on the show to donating to the animal shelter...it couldn't have happened without you."

"Oh, Blythe," Zoe said, feeling a little embarrassed. "*Everybody* worked hard to make this happen."

"But it was all *your* idea," Blythe told her as she leaned down to give Zoe a giant hug. "And no one worked harder than you."

And that made Zoe really feel like a star!

Read on for a preview of another Littlest Pet Shop book, *Project FUN-way: Starring Russell Ferguson!*

Who's calling me in the middle of the night? Blythe wondered sleepily as she reached for the phone. She pressed the answer button and mumbled, "Hello?"

"*Blythe,* darling, how *are* you?"

Blythe sat up straighter, completely wide awake. There was no mistaking that voice—it was the one and only Mona Autumn, publisher of the world-famous fashion magazine *Tres Blasé*. Mona was a glittering star in the fashion world, and Blythe had been in awe of her ever since Blythe sketched her very first fashion design.

Everybody knew that Blythe loved fashion, especially designing her own unique outfits. But what people *didn't* know was that Blythe had a top secret ability that she would never, ever reveal to anyone. Blythe could communicate with animals! At first, Blythe was incredibly freaked out by her unusual talent, but as she got used to it, Blythe started to understand just how amazing it was to understand animals, especially her pet friends. Not only could she help them when other people couldn't, but the pets could help Blythe whenever she needed them. She and the pets had had so many amazing adventures together—including a recent trip to the international Pet Fashion Expo, where Blythe and one of her pet pals, Russell the hedgehog, had been photographed for *Tres Blasé*! That was how Blythe had managed to meet someone as important and influential as Mona Autumn.

"I'm calling from Paris with the most fabulous news," Mona said briskly. "Are you sitting down, Blythe? Because you really should be sitting down."

Does lying down count? Blythe wondered. But before she could reply, Mona continued.

"Our latest issue of *Tres Blasé*—yes, that's right, the one with you and your prickly pet— has sold more than half a million copies!"

Blythe gasped. Half a million copies? That news wasn't just fantastic—it was amazing. Astonishing. Unbelievable!

"Half a million copies?" Blythe repeated, still in shock.

"And still selling! We simply can't print them fast enough!" Mona crowed. "Needless to say, *everyone's* thrilled. The fashion industry's thrilled. Our advertisers are thrilled. Even *I'm* thrilled—and I am *very* hard to thrill."

"I'm so—" Blythe started, but once more, Mona kept talking.

"And the public! The public is *beyond* thrilled! What they want, Blythe, is more. More Blythe Style, more fashion hedgehog, more *Tres Blasé*, more, more, more! And do you know what we're going to do?"

This time, Blythe didn't even try to answer.

"We're going to give it to them!" Mona answered her own question. "That's where you come in. We want you and Russell as the headline stars for a very special event being held in Paris in ten days!"

"A fashion show?" Blythe was so excited her voice sounded all squeaky.

"Better," Mona declared. "A fashion show at the first-ever Everyday Hero Awards, right on the runway at the Paris airport!"